THE
OLD SOUL'S
HANDBOOK

Also by Michelle Gordon:

Fiction
The Girl Who Loved Too Much

Earth Angel Series
The Earth Angel Training Academy
The Earth Angel Awakening
The Other Side
The Twin Flame Reunion
The Twin Flame Retreat
The Twin Flame Resurrection
The Twin Flame Reality
The Twin Flame Rebellion
The Twin Flame Reignition
The Twin Flame Resolution

Visionary Collection
Heaven dot com
The Doorway to PAM
The Elphite
I'm Here

Poetry
Duelling Poets

Non-fiction
Where's My F**king Unicorn?

THE OLD SOUL'S HANDBOOK

MICHELLE GORDON

First published in Limited Edition Hardback in Great Britain in 2018 by The Amethyst Angel
Second Edition Published in Great Britain in 2020 by The Amethyst Angel

The Amethyst Angel is an imprint of
Not From This Planet

ISBN: 978-1-912257-21-8

Second Edition

This book is for every Earth Angel I have met on my
journey.

I love every single one of you.

My Dear Earth Angel,

So many times you have lamented on how you wish there was a handbook for living this human life on Earth, containing wisdom and advice that woud get you through the strangest and toughest times of your existence.

Well here it is. Every quote in this book is from the ten books in the Earth Angel Series. They have been sorted into themes, and so you can either go to the theme you are having issues with and then read the quotes in that section for wisdom, or you can ask a question, flick through the pages and stop in a random place for the answer.

Even if the quote appears to make no sense in relation to your question, allow it to properly sink in and then let go, as the meaning may well be revealed at a later stage.

Nothing in this book is to be taken as medical, legal or financial advice, and indeed, many of the quotes will appear to contradict one another. If you act on any of the wisdom within these pages, then the consequences of your actions are entirely your responsibility.

Having said that, I do hope that you find comfort within these pages, and that you find joy and happinesss even in the darkest moments you may experience on this planet.

All my love,
Velvet.

x

LOVE

The strength of your love for her overrides
everything.

Logic, reason, knowledge, and wisdom are
all meaningless when stood face to face
with your love, your emotions and your
connection to your Twin Flame.

Which is exactly how it should be.

On Earth, there would seem to be many different types of love.

You love your mother, you love the sunshine, you love to read, you love chocolate ice cream.

But honestly, there is only one kind of love.

We just express that love in different ways and in different amounts.

Twin Flames are one with each other forever.

No matter how much time and distance may appear to be separating them.

Because of course, the separation is an illusion.

Your capacity to love unconditionally means
you do not need to have a Twin Flame
connection to experience that kind of love.

When our bodies entwine, our souls become
one and there is nowhere else on this planet
I would rather be

Even if he had a hundred years with her, he didn't feel like it would be enough to know everything about her.

I know that my purpose is not living a long life with my Flame, but to Awaken the world.

I love you.
I love you with everything I have.
But what if that's not enough?
Or what if it's too much?

You cannot let go.

And you're not meant to.

That is not the nature of Twin Flames.

They are one with each other forever.

No matter how much time and distance may
appear to be separating them.

Because of course, the separation is an
illusion.

I love him, but he's not my Flame.

You are.

We came here together, we are meant to be together.

I love you.

I just need to work out what my purpose is
now.

Maybe your purpose is to love me.

Maybe it is.

I'll love you for eternity.

Our love will outlast eternity itself.

I have changed my fate, and yours.

We won't have to say good bye now.

It's a beautiful thing, to find your other half,
your one true mate.

I feel… complete.

Like my soul is filled with love and joy and light. I feel like I want to sing and dance and just hold him all night and all day.

Gag me.
I think everyone around here has gone mad
with all this Twin Flame stuff.
Love at first sight?
Oh, please!
Everyone just wants to get some!

She looked forward to the simple pleasure
of meeting someone, falling in love and
spending every moment possible in their
embrace.

She knew it wasn't always that simple, but
the difficulties of being human were always
so much easier to bear, it seemed, when you
were loved by another.

Listen to yourself.
Listen to the Angels whispering to you.
Listen to music and listen to the sounds of
nature. All of the answers you seek can be
found if you just ask the right question, then
listen for the answer.
Listen. And you will Awaken.
Listen, and you will find yourself again.
Listen, and you will find your Twin Flame,
your soulmate.
Listen, and you will always find your way
home again.

She was sad to lose another friend, but there was nothing she could do to stop it. She hoped that one day he would forgive her for not returning his feelings.

I would tell you not to worry, that the Universe will bring you and your Flame together, that you will of course spend a good part of your life with your Twin, but the truth is, I don't know that.

I can only hope that it will indeed happen.

I hope you, too, are reunited with your
Flame.

She really hoped the two of them came to their senses soon.

It seemed so crazy to have Twin Flames in such close proximity to one another who wouldn't admit their true feelings.

I hope that wherever you are, whomever you are with; you are happy.

I had hoped to see you again, but I don't think it will be possible.

It is a difficult thing, to forget such love.

It is time for those on Earth to experience love in the way that it was intended.

To be with the other half of their very souls.

We are hoping that this kind of love will produce the miracles that the world so desperately needs.

She felt such an immense feeling of love when she thought about him. Like she had been lost, alone and living in a dull, grey world when suddenly, she looked into his eyes and everything exploded with colour.

I honestly believe that the unions between
the Flames will bring more love to the
world than has been seen for the last two
thousand years of this human age.

I love you. I always have.
During all of the lifetimes we have known
each other, I have been in love with you.

A misconception about love is that it can be exchanged between beings, given away, lost or found.

Love, isn't an object. It isn't merely an emotion, either: it is pure energy.

It is the feeling that we experience when we are in sync with the Universe. When we are flowing with the river of life.

Let yourself melt, transform, be transfigured into another state of being. When you do, you will be in love with the world. Not to mention the fact that you will be outwardly happy, and contented. Which, in accordance with the law of attraction, will bring you more people, things and circumstances that will help you to feel the love within.

Her heart was so full at times she thought it would burst. Every touch, every kiss, every whisper in her ear, made her heart skip a beat.

I know it now.
I know that he is my Twin Flame.
Without a shadow of a doubt.

Love like this was most definitely the kind of love that could perform miracles.

It may only have been for a short time, but you were together; you did have your final Twin Flame relationship on Earth.

Those times you spent together, the love that you felt when in their arms, it was all real, I promise.

The thing with saying goodbye, is that no matter how many times you say it, it still always hurts as much as it did the first time.

You are a beautiful, perfect soul, and I will love you unconditionally forever.

Our love is like the stars shining above:
infinite, everlasting, radiant; glowing
brightly in the darkness, never fading away.

One thing she knew for certain was that
whether they reunited in this lifetime or not,
she would always love him deeply.
For eternity.

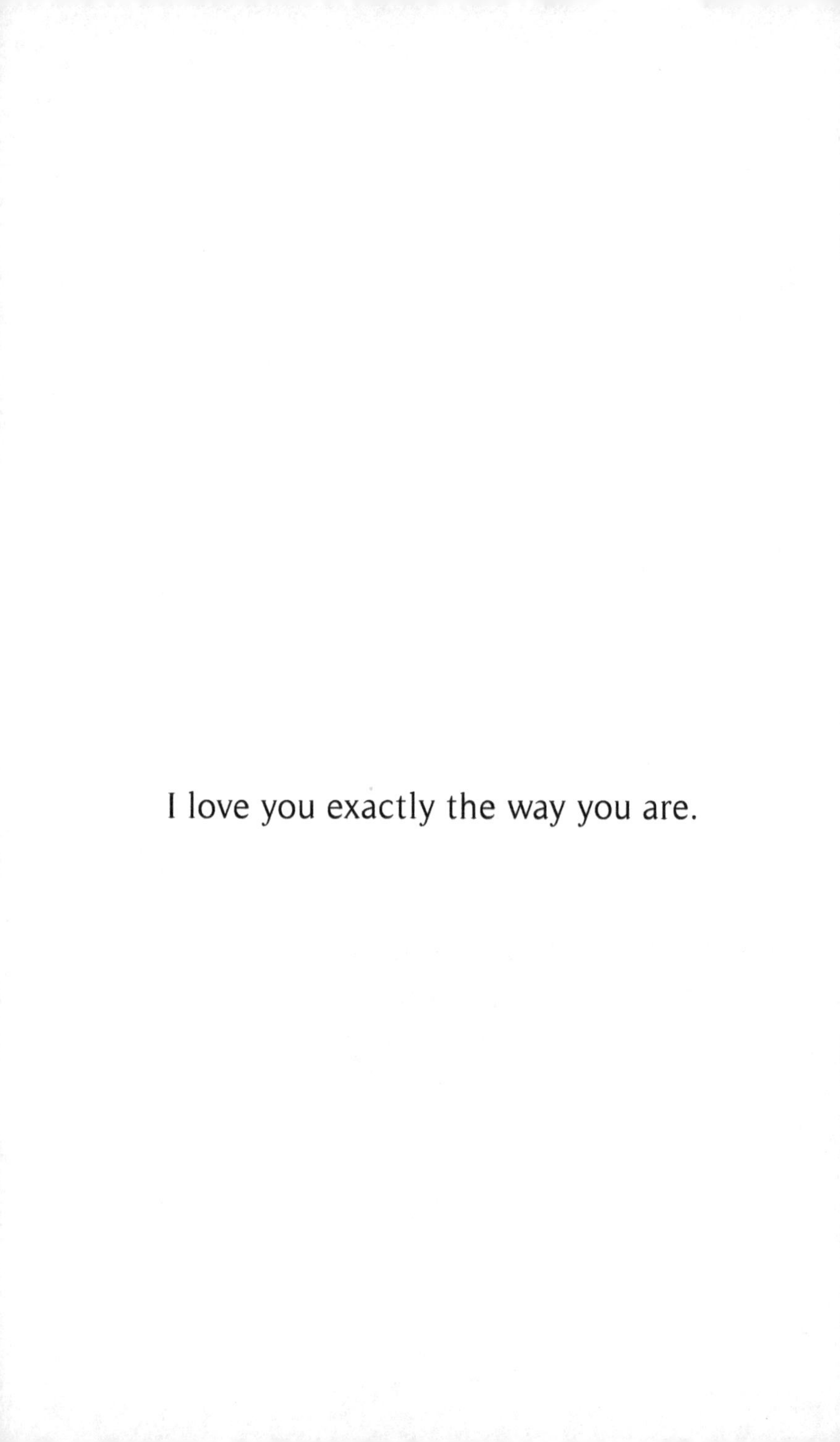

I love you exactly the way you are.

He had felt for a while that this moment would come, that they would need to part ways, not because they had fallen out of love, or because they hated each other, or because either of them had found someone else.

But because it was the right thing for their soul missions.

She realised now that it would be better to be alone than to be with someone whom she didn't love with every molecule of her heart and soul.

I love you. I love you more than anything or
anyone else in the Universe. I want to spend
all my earthly moments with you before
we go to the stars together. I don't see how
there could be any possible reason why us
being apart is for the good of all humanity
or for us, and I will do whatever it takes to
be with you.

With a clear heart and mind, I have found
that I love you, absolutely, unconditionally
and unequivocally.

DEATH

Our connection goes beyond this world, and
goes back further than we can imagine.
It's eternal.
As we are all eternal.
We are one.

Sometimes we manage to save them, sometimes we're not so lucky. Instead of thinking they have died, I like to think they have gone home to the ocean. I know it's where I'll be headed one day.

My Flame left me too. And it was the end of my world. I didn't want to exist on this planet without him, but, ultimately, going home wasn't the answer. Because I had family, and friends who loved me, who would have missed me so much. And because it is possible find happiness and fulfil your purpose on Earth without your Flame. You are enough as you are.

Don't cry, my love.
We are one.
This separation is nothing but an illusion, for
I am with you always.

My dear, sweet Child. There is no such thing
as death. You will simply be going home.

A soul had once told her that he knew if he ignored the whispers of the Angels, he was sure to return home.

I couldn't lose you. I would follow you anywhere in the Universe rather than lose you.

Though it had been such a long time, he could still smell her hair. He could still hear her laughter. He could still see her smile. He wished he could see her again. Talk to her. Apologise to her for not saving her.

It's just been so hard. I couldn't breathe
without him. I couldn't sleep or eat.
Everything just hurt so much. And I know it
seems crazy, it's not like we'd been together
for long, but he was my other half. I just
couldn't see the point in continuing without
him.

Nothing lasts forever.

Even if this is the end, it will all work out just fine. There is nothing to fear, no darkness to endure, nothing to lose.

Death is simply another part of life.
You still exist, you are still with me.

I know we will be together again.
Do not fear, I will watch over you always.

What will I do without you? You are my guiding star, my shining light in the heavens.

I will not be so far away. You will be within me, as I am within you, always.

Have I not said before?
That this separation is but an illusion?
We are one. We are never apart.

The pain of being so far from your light has caused me to dwell on the darkness.

I don't know how to do this,
I don't know if I can.

We'll do it together

The world has not lost their light.
The ripples of the love they gave and the
incredible work they did will continue to
grow for a long time yet.

It always seems so cruel when two people
who love each other so deeply get to spend
so little time together.

Death is, well, quite beautiful actually.
The shedding of the heavy human body,
then the shedding of all worries, troubles,
fear; it's like being reborn as a beautiful
divine spark of light.
It is being reunited with the Universe, the
illusion of separation is shattered and you
feel whole again.
Death is the discovery of pure love.

Listen to your heart, and you will always
find me

Whatever you do, don't put your life on hold.
Live.

I'll check in on you from time to time.

Nothing terrible could possibly happen
because I knew that death wasn't terrible.
Dying was simply a way to get home.

Once fear overtakes a soul, and shuts the love and light out, then that person is merely tiptoeing through life so that they can die from old age.
Life is to be experienced, to be filled with joy and happiness.
Not wasted by being dull.

Death, after all, does not exist.

Death, it seems, is no way to escape.

It's a difficult thing, saying goodbye.
Even when you know that it's only for a
short time.

Why must it always end this way? Why must
it end at all?

So it may begin again.

I'm going to miss you. In all this time, I don't think I've ever truly told you how much I love you.

I have also come to realise, that alive on Earth, or in spirit here, or among the stars – the pain of losing a Twin Flame never fades.

He wished that there was something he
could say to soothe her.
But he also knew that letting go and
learning how to say goodbye was an
important lesson.

I can remember what it feels like, to lose a loved one. It must be the hardest thing I ever experienced as a human.

It may never end, it may go on forever.
As you may go on forever.

BEAUTY

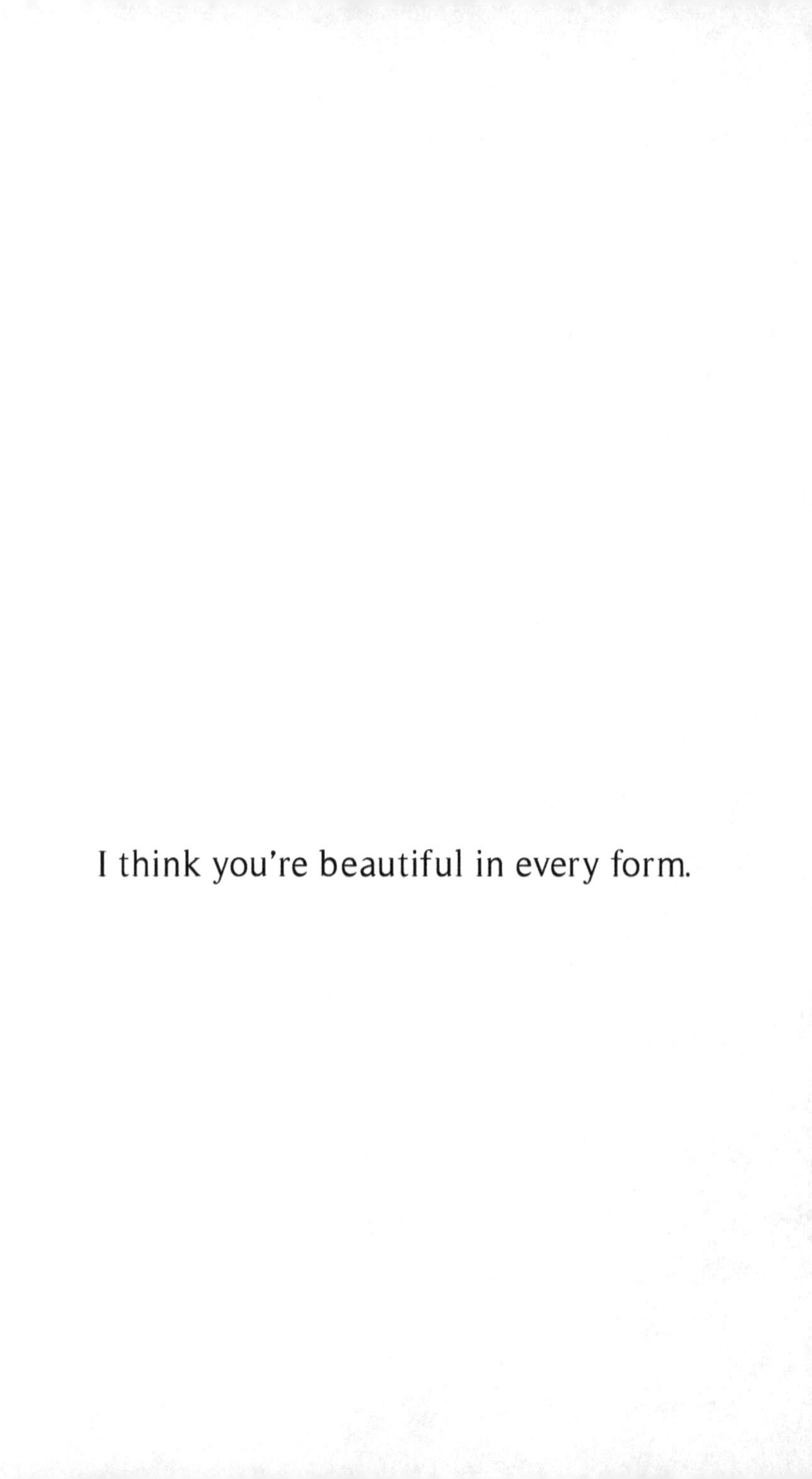

I think you're beautiful in every form.

You will look beautiful at every stage of your life, I have no doubt about that.

It's like there's been a whole side of the world that I have just never noticed before. And you have opened my eyes to it.

Life, as a human on Earth, is not always a
beautiful experience.
Some of it is ugly and painful.

Sometimes the most selfish acts are also the
most beautiful.

You may just be one drop in the ocean, but you are a very beautiful drop.

Your Earthly beauty cannot hold a candle to
your true self, but you are beautiful all the
same.

It's about finding beauty in ordinary things.
Really noticing the world around you.
It's difficult at times, to see the good when
the bad is shouting in our faces, but it can
be done. Just watching a leaf falling from a
tree, a bird building its nest or feeling the
rain on your face can cleanse your soul of
the darkness.

The idea of inspiring people to wake up to
the beauty of the world was both exciting
and terrifying and overwhelming all at the
same time.

HOPE

I admire your courage, your strength, and
your ability to love so deeply.
It gives me hope.

Nothing is ever lost.
Everything is connected.
Anything is possible

Do not trouble yourself with the difficulties we face on Earth, focus instead on the beautiful missions we have come here to accomplish.

Even the smallest person can make a
difference.

If we can bring love, light and peace to just one human being, we will have made a difference.

I hope the aliens know what they're letting
themselves in for.

It is good to see that so many still have faith
in the power of the shift.

Let's hope our faith proves true.

Hopefully, humans will begin to understand
that being different is not only acceptable,
but it is something to be proud of.

We must remember that every drop creates ripples that spread outwards, reaching far and wide, despite its small original size. Each of us will be a single drop, but the ripples we create will hopefully reach many, many humans, connect us to other Earth Angels, and help the ripples to reach every corner of the Earth.

I know it may seem that our mission is
hopeless. That all of us going back to Earth
may not change anything at all.
But I think the point is that we try.

I shouldn't have given up.

No matter how overcast the sky, the stars continue to shine.

We just have to be patient enough to wait for the clouds to lift.

TIME

Time passes so slowly it feels as though
every moment is an eternity.
Which in fact it is, seeing as all of time is an
illusion, and all that exists is this moment.

Life is so transitional, so temporary.
We really have no idea what is going to
happen from moment to moment.
All we can do is enjoy the
moment we are experiencing

Everything happens for a reason and
everything happens in the perfect sequence.

How could everything change in such a small
amount of time?

Now, are you ready?

I can go right now?

'Now' is all that exists, remember?

I've wasted too much time doing nothing.
I need to take action.
I'm not going to waste another minute.

We feel that souls are still holding onto the belief that it takes time to invent, time to create things. That things don't just appear as a result of thought. The issue with this is that it's taking too long for things to be invented and created that will shift the world toward the Golden Age.

OBSTACLES

Interruptions and obstacles are good. Without them, we would be on a never-ending, straight and boring path.

It's a weird collision between the eternal
ethereal realm and the illusionary physical
realm we find ourselves in.

You have allowed it to grip you.
You have welcomed the darkness in.
Because truly that is the only way it can
affect you in this way; with your invitation
for it to do so.
You could choose, in an instant, to stop
letting it affect you, to have no impact on
you, and it would be so.

Every time I think I've got it figured out, it
seems to change.

You mustn't lose hope!
It sounds bleak and I know that the human world is filled with despair, sadness and anger.
But it is also filled with wonder and joy and love and happiness.

Why is it that even though we can be so excited to go somewhere, it is still somehow difficult to leave?

Because though you are moving forward into new and exciting adventures, you'll still always love what you have left behind.

I would never say there was no reason for it.
There is a reason for everything.

Your fire no longer burns as brightly, but you must keep fanning the flames until they return.
It is important.

She no longer felt a heaviness in her heart;
she no longer felt trapped by her own
longing and loneliness.
Somehow, she felt as though she had been
set free, and now her overwhelming desire
was to do something with this new feeling
of freedom.

Forget the how, focus on the what.
The how is for God to figure out.

Just because your day begins badly, doesn't mean it has to stay at the same level all day. You can consciously change your energy vibration.

Do you think it was effortless in the
beginning?
Do you think I found it easy?
Do you think it all worked out perfectly?
Of course not.
But I had faith that everything would begin
to harmonise, and that it would work out
perfectly in the end.

Now is not the time to hide. The world is
getting darker, angrier, and more violent.
It needs you to stand up and bring light
into the darkness, not hide in the shadows,
hoping not to be noticed.

HEALING

It is possible to heal anything,
you know that.

I am powerful.

I am healthy.

I am love.

I deserve the best.

I am open to the good of the Universe.

I promise I will be with you every step of the way, and I will do whatever I can to help with your healing.

I think entering a more spiritual way of life can help. And different practices like meditation, or healing can also help. But there are many healthy ways to find peace. Walking, running, writing, painting, making love.

It's time to put your own wellbeing first.
I can see you've lost your sparkle.

DREAMS

Crazy dreams of a million stars in the sky,
and laying on a field of nothing but four-
leafed clovers.

Doubts kill dreams.
Kill doubt, not dreams.

I realise that not everyone gets the
opportunity for another chance like
this, and I realise that I may not actually
deserve it. But it's something that I believe,
wholeheartedly, I need to do.

Bring me beautiful dreams, Angels.

She was desperate to sleep, so she could escape the nightmare into her dreams.

FREE WILL

Do you really believe there is such a thing as being in the wrong place at the wrong time? Or indeed being in the right place at the right time? Everything that happens in a human's life happens because of his or her own choices. There is no such thing as chance, fate or luck - just choices.

The beauty of free will and choice is this –
when a human is experiencing something
undesirable in their life, they get to choose
how they experience it. They can choose
to be upset, angry or miserable, which is
perfectly acceptable, or they can choose to
see it as an opportunity to grow, to realise
their own strength or as a time to end what
they knew before and to begin again.

Life does not need to be easy.
It does not need to be hard, either.
As a human, you get to choose which it is.
Your perception of events is your experience
of events.
It is entirely in your hands.

You know you cannot go against the law of
free will.
They haven't asked for your help.

All souls have free will.
You are here of your own will.

It's more difficult to affect others with our manifestations.

I wish I could tell you that it'll all work out, but I can't. It doesn't work like that. Predicting a person's life path isn't like predicting the weather. Just one tiny decision, a change of mind, a change of timing even, can change the entire course of someone's life.

There is no such thing as the right path.
There are many paths, you choose one and
you see what happens. If you don't like
where the path leads, then you follow a new
one.

It is time for souls on Earth to make definite
decisions, to move forward with clarity,
not just stumble along on a path they think
might be the right one for them.

You fought for me, you fought for our love.
And in that moment, you changed the world.

Time is irrelevant, and how long you have
been a certain way is irrelevant.
The only thing that is relevant is whether
you are motivated enough to first of all
decide to change, and then to make those
changes happen.

AWAKENING

Choosing to be an Earth Angel means that
you are choosing to go to Earth to bring
peace and love to humans and help them to
Awaken to the reality.

That is a near impossible task if you keep
to yourself and refuse to step out into the
spotlight.

We have to retain as much love and light as
we can, so that when we're on Earth, we
can shine brightly, and encourage others to
shine too.

I think that in the next few years, people will begin to believe in magick again. They will come alive again, and shake off the illusion they've been trapped in.

Humans are beginning to understand that there is so much out there that is unknown and even magickal in nature, and they are becoming more accepting.

I believe that the shift in consciousness will make humans more spiritual, more aware than they have ever been before.

That very morning, in fact, she had awoken
with the feeling that today would be a big
day. That something was going to enter her
existence, and possibly change the future of
the world.

Awakening can be a difficult process. And because it is human nature to crave acceptance and love, being openly different can be a painful and terrifying thing. If you manage to remember one thing, let it be this – do not crave acceptance from others, only wish to understand and accept yourself. Be yourself, and you will be a success. Try to become someone else, and you will have forgotten your own soul.

Really go into your heart, your soul, and listen only to your inner voice. Ignore any outside whispering. Go within. You know the truth, you know who you really love and where you really want to be.

She knew that she was making a difference.
She was making history.
She was Awakening the world.

We're becoming more aware and Awake, and we're realising that it's impossible for us to be here and live lives full of passion and purpose if we're around someone who drains us of our energy.

Art makes a huge difference, as does music and literature. The energetic vibration of what we create makes a big difference to the world as a whole. We can uplift, inspire, and cause a range of emotions to be felt through our work. So if you infuse the intention of love, light and Awakening into your pieces, you will be fulfilling your mission.

HAPPINESS

I would like to wish you all the love and
happiness in the Universe.
May your human life be everything you hope
it to be.

You need to remain open to the
opportunities that come your way.
If you get a gut feeling to do something,
then do it.
If your inner voice is urging you to go a
certain way, even if it's not the normal way,
then go.

Happiness doesn't come from owning or attaining things or people, it comes from the place deep inside where you are secure in the knowledge that everything is exactly as it should be.

Everything happens for a reason, and instead of labelling it good or bad, we should appreciate it for how it changes our lives.

Focus on feeling happy.
The more you focus on the feeling of
happiness, the more things will come along
that make you feel happy.

One of the main problems is not that we don't have what we want, but that we don't know what we want. And if **we** don't know, then how is the Universe supposed to know?

The pain was necessary.
As all pain was necessary.
Without it, how could joy possibly be
known?

I know that you can do this, that you have more love and happiness yet to experience in this lifetime.

Who would choose the pain and darkness and struggle over an eternal life of light and joy?

Him, apparently.

We believe that the joy of being human is
the uncertainty and unpredictability of life

I never understood why people married each other out of convenience, or a sense of duty or out of loneliness. That's not the path to happiness.

I agree. You do it for true, unconditional love, or you die as a bachelor or a cat lady.

Exactly.

When we look for happiness or love outside
of ourselves, before finding it within,
whatever we find will never be sustainable.

The answers you seek are within you, my
love.

You need not seek the answers outside of
yourself. You know that.

FRIENDSHIP

You have been a true friend to me, and I
want you to know just how much I love you.

Do you think I'm being silly?

**No. I think you're just being a good friend.
Though I do love a good bit of silliness.**

Being in a Twin Flame relationship can be really intense, and it can be too easy to become so wrapped up in each other that it's difficult to make time for others. But it is important to take the time to continue nurturing relationships and friendships outside of the Twin Flame union, and to give each other the space to explore and evolve too.

DESTINY

You know that nothing could possibly change the ultimate outcome.

Oh well. I suppose we should just enjoy the show then.

That's not a bad philosophy to have in life.

There are no such things as coincidences.
Anything that seems like one has happened
deliberately.

We choose our futures with every word spoken, action taken or thought in our minds. It's not always a conscious choice. In fact, most of us would appear to have chosen the exact future that we did not want to experience, but because our thoughts have been so heavily focused on that which we do not want, that is the future we experience.

Destiny is such a fragile thing, isn't it?

ABOUT THE AUTHOR

Michelle lives in the UK, when she's not flitting in and out of other realms. She believes in Faeries and Unicorns and thinks the world needs more magic and fun in it. She writes because she would go crazy if she didn't. She might already be a little crazy, so please buy more books so she can keep writing.

Please feel free to write a review of this book. Michelle loves to get direct feedback, so if you would like to contact her, please e-mail theamethystangel@hotmail.co.uk or keep up to date by following her blog – **TwinFlameBlog.com**. You can also follow her on Twitter **@themiraclemuse** or or on Instagram **@michellegordonauthor**

You can now become an Earth Angel Trainee:
earthangelacademy.co.uk

To sign up to her mailing list, visit:
michellegordon.co.uk

BOOKS BY MICHELLE GORDON

WHERE'S MY F**KING UNICORN?

Are your bookshelves filled with self-help books, and yet your life feels empty? Do you keep following paths to enlightenment that lead to the same dead ends? You've read the books, attended the seminars and taken heed of every bit of advice going... but you're still waiting for your f**king unicorn to come along! Where's My F**king Unicorn? is a guide to life, creativity and happiness that offers a very different way forward. Author, Michelle Gordon, explains why, in spite of all your best efforts, your life still doesn't live up to your vision of what it should be, and tells you exactly what you can do about it. In refreshingly down-to-earth language, she shows you how to harness all the self-knowledge you have gained from all those self-help books you've read, and actually start putting it to practical use.

Where's My F**king Unicorn? is published by *Ammonite Press* and is available online and in bookstores.

Earth Angel Series

The Earth Angel Training Academy
(book 1)

There are humans on Earth, who are not, in fact, human.

They are **Earth Angels**.

Earth Angels are beings who have come from other realms,
dimensions and planets, and are choosing to be born on
Earth in human form for just **one** reason.

To **Awaken the world**.

Before they can carry out their perilous mission, they must
first learn how to be human.

The best place they can do that, is at
The Earth Angel Training Academy

The Earth Angel Awakening
(book 2)

After learning how to be human at the Earth Angel Training
Academy, the Angels, Faeries, Merpeople and Starpeople are
born into human bodies on Earth.

Their Mission? **Awaken the world**.

But even though they **chose** to go to Earth, and they chose
to be human, it doesn't mean that it will be **easy** for them
to Awaken themselves.

Only if they **reconnect** to their **origins**,
and to other Earth Angels, will they will be able to
remember who they really are.

Only then, will they experience
The Earth Angel Awakening

THE OTHER SIDE
(book 3)

There is an Angel who holds the world in her hands.
She is the **Angel of Destiny**.
Her actions will start the **ripples** that will **save humans**
from their certain demise.
In order for her to initiate the necessary changes, she
must travel to other **galaxies**, and call upon the most
enlightened and **evolved** beings of the Universe.
To save **humankind**.
When they agree, she wishes to prepare them for Earth
life, and so invites them to attend the Earth Angel Training
Academy, on
The Other Side

THE TWIN FLAME REUNION
(book 4)

The Earth Angels' missions are clear: **Awaken** the world,
and move humanity into the **Golden Age**.
But there is another reason many of the Earth Angels
choose to come to Earth.
To **reunite** with their **Twin Flames**.
The Twin Flame connection is deep, everlasting and intense,
and happens only at the **end of an age**. Many Flames
have not been together for millennia, some have never met.
Once on Earth, every Earth Angel longs to meet their
Flame. The one who will make them **feel at home**, who
will make living on this planet bearable.
But no one knows if they will actually get to experience
The Twin Flame Reunion

The Twin Flame Retreat
(book 5)

The question in the minds of many Earth Angels
on Earth right now is:
Where is my **Twin Flame?**
Though many Earth Angels are now meeting their Flames,
the circumstances around their reunion can have
life-altering consequences.
If meeting your Flame meant your life would never be the
same again, would you still want to find them?
When in need of **support** and answers,
Earth Angels attend
The Twin Flame Retreat

The Twin Flame Resurrection
(book 6)

Twin Flames are **destined** to meet. And when they are
meant to be together, nothing can keep them apart.
Not even **death**.
When Earth Angels go home to the Fifth Dimension too
soon, they have the **choice** to come back.
To be with their **Twin Flame**.
The connection can be so overwhelming, that some Earth
Angels try to resist it, try to push it away.
But it is **undeniable**.
When things don't go according to plan, the universe steps
in, and the Earth Angels experience
The Twin Flame Ressurrection

THE TWIN FLAME REALITY
(book 7)

Being an Earth Angel on Earth can be difficult, especially
when it doesn't feel like home, and when there's a deep
longing for a realm or dimension where you feel you
belong.
Finding a Twin Flame, is like **coming home**.
Losing one, can be **devastating**.
Adrift, lonely, isolated... an Earth Angel would be forgiven
for preferring to go home, than to stay here
without their Flame.
But if they can find the **strength** to stay, to follow their
mission to **Awaken** the world, and fulfil their original
purpose, they will find they can be **happy** here.
Even despite the sadness of
The Twin Flame Reality

THE TWIN FLAME REBELLION
(book 8)

The Angels on the Other Side have a **duty** to **help** their
human charges, but **only** when they are **asked** for help.
They are not allowed to meddle with **Free Will**.
But a number of Angels are asked to break their
Golden Rule, and start influencing the human
lives of the Earth Angels.
Once the Angels start nudging, they find they can't stop, and
when the Earth Angels find out they are being manipulated
from the Other Side, they aren't happy.
Determined to **choose** their own **fate**,
the Earth Angels embark on
The Twin Flame Rebellion

THE TWIN FLAME REIGNITION
(book 9)

The **destiny** of many **Twin Flames** is changing.
Those destined to remain apart on Earth are hearing the
call to come **together.**
As things begin to shift and change, it suddenly it seems
possible for them to **reunite,** and have the lives they
always **dreamed** of.
But when **visions** and **dreams** of **Atlantis** begin to
plague the Earth Angels, and they try to work out their
meaning, what they **discover** may jeopardise
The Twin Flame Reignition

THE TWIN FLAME RESOLUTION
(book 10)

When a Seer has a **vision** of the **Golden Age**, she takes
drastic action in order to make it happen.
The consequences of her actions are so **epic** that the lives
of every **Earth Angel** and every **human** on Earth will
be altered **forever.**
As well as the unions of all the
Twin Flames.
She enlists the help of two **Angels** to assist her in
The Twin Flame Resolution

The Earth Angel Series is published by
The Amethyst Angel and is available online in eBook and print.

Visionary Collection

Heaven dot com

When Christina goes into hospital for the final time, and knows that she is about to lose her battle with cancer, she asks her boyfriend, James, to help her deliver messages to her family and friends after she has gone.

She also asks him to do something for her, but she dies before he can make it happen, and he finds it difficult to forgive himself.

After her death, her messages are received by her loved ones, and the impact her words have will change their lives forever.

The Doorway to PAM

Natalie is an ordinary girl who has lost her way. There is nothing particularly special about her or her life. She has no exceptional abilities. She hasn't achieved anything miraculous. Her life has very little meaning to it.

Evelyn is the caretaker at Pam's. The alternate dimension where souls at their lowest point find the answers they need to turn their lives around. The dimension dreamers visit, to help people while they sleep.

One ordinary girl, one extraordinary woman.
One fated meeting that will change lives.

The Elphite

Ellie's life is just one long, bad case of déjà vu. She has lived her life before - a hundred times before - and she remembers each and every lifetime.
Each time, she has changed things, but has never managed to change the ending.
This time, in this life, she hopes that it will be different.
So she makes the biggest change of all - she tries to avoid meeting him.
Her soulmate. The love of her life.
Because maybe if they don't meet, she can finally change her destiny.
But fate has other ideas...

I'm Here

When Marielle finds out that a guy she had a crush on in school has passed away, the strange occurrences of the previous week begin to make sense. She suspects that he is trying to give her a message from the other side, and so opens up to communicate with him, She has no idea that by doing so, she will be forming a bond so strong, that life as she knows it will forever be changed.

Nathan assumed that when he died, he would move on, and continue his spiritual journey. But instead he finds himself drawn to a girl that he once knew. The more he watches her, and gets to know her, he realises that he was drawn to her for a reason, and that once he knows what that is, he will be able to change his destiny.

The Visionary Collection is published by
The Amethyst Angel and is available online in eBook and print.

LITTLE SOMETHING

by Elizabeth Lockwood

Waiting for a little something…A motivational memoir which is as real as it is miraculous. After getting married, trying for a baby was the next logical step. But nothing happened. Nothing. Months and months of nothing. Medical tests showed that there were issues on both sides and treatment would be required to even have a small chance of getting pregnant. But with almost 100 pounds of weight loss standing in the way, Elizabeth Lockwood just couldn't see how it would be possible. But it was, and after losing weight, IVF treatment became a reality. Two treatment cycles later, and no baby, Elizabeth turned to running to aid her mental health. In training for marathons she found a positive way to move forward.But then it all changed… Little Something is about hopes, dreams, and resilience. Finding ways to illuminate the darkness, and never ever giving up. Oh, and the miracles that occur when you least expect them.

Little Something is published by *Labradorite Press* and is available online in eBook and print.

THE MAGICAL FAERIE DOOR
by Michelle Louise Gordon

*The magical full moon
lights the doorway to Eireaf,
land of the purple sun
and the golden faerie queen*

Lily believes in faeries.

She always has. Even though she had never seen one.
Because she believes that there is still magic in the world.

And because the magic inside her is recognised, she is led
to the faerie realm, where she is given a very important
mission...

The Magical Faerie Door is published by *Amber Beetle Books* and
is available online in eBook and hardback.

Duelling Poets

For 30 days in 2012, Michelle Gordon and Victor Keegan wrote a poem a day, taking turns to choose the titles.

Michelle is an author, who was in her late 20s at the time, and Victor, a retired journalist in his 70s. Their differing experiences and perspectives created contrasting poems, despite being written about the same topic.

In Duelling Poets, we invite you to read the poems and choose your favourites, then at the end, you can see which poet wins the duel for you.

Duelling Poets is published by *Turquoise Quill Press* and is available online in eBook and print.

Not From This Planet is an Independent Publisher on a mission to collaborate with authors to create the best possible books that delight and inspire and entertain – and also pay a fair royalty to the author. They treat every book as if it were their own and they have big have plans to take the publishing world by storm.

Follow Not From This Planet on
Instagram - @notfromthisplanetbooks
Facebook - @notfromthisplanetbooks
Twitter - @ NFTPbooks

NotFromThisPlanet.co.uk

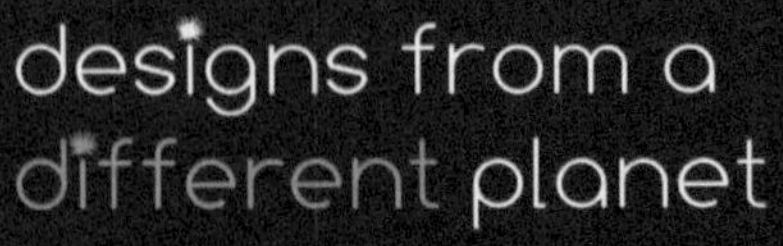

designs from a
different planet

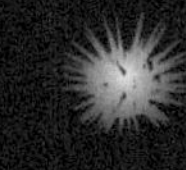

madappledesigns
.co.uk